ISBN: 978-0-9786352-3-7

Printed in the United States of America

Book Design and Illustration: Christopher M. Rogers

For more information and to order more copies, visit
us at: www.HomerTheHelicopter.com

Dedicated to my beloved mother
Neca J. Watts
teacher and eternal optimist

 # Chapter 1

Bang! . . . bang! . . . bang! Buzz-z-z-z-z. Splash, swoosh, splash-h-h-h . . . The sounds of hammers, saws, and paint echoed throughout the giant factory. When the noises finally stopped, a squeaky hoist lowered something slowly to the ground. Ooohs and ahhhs moved through the crowd. It had taken many months for the workmen to shape Homer's body into a perfect flying machine. And now, Homer the helicopter was being born right in the middle of the factory's scrap heap.

Unlike other newborn helicopters who were timid and made fussing noises, Homer was brave from the start. His shiny skin was cut from the finest silver metal. And on top of the little 'copter sat two sparkling new blades. As the blades began to spin, Homer felt a gentle wind above his head. With each quickening turn of his new propeller, Homer's emerald green eyes danced and flashed even brighter, and his smile turned to a wide grin. The dimples in each corner of his mouth and on his chin deepened with delight and his stubby nose stuck out like a silver jewel.

It was time for the factory workmen to turn Homer over to his mother, the wise, golden-colored Elsa. She was elegant with six glowing lights on her frame. On top of her huge blades sat a brilliant strobe light that twirled around, brightly flashing on and off.

Elsa had waited a long time to raise a son just like Homer. She was so thrilled and proud of her new son that she took him in tow behind her and flew around the factory in a precise, zigzag flight pattern. Elsa wanted to show off Homer to all the other mothers who had come to celebrate the little 'copter's arrival into the world.

Elsa was a graceful flyer, and under her guidance the two of them drifted lightly through the air like floating swans.

After several minutes, Homer became restless and decided to play a prank on his mother. When Elsa zigged, Homer zagged in the opposite direction. Again and again the rope swiftly jerked him backward, each time giving the

little helicopter a thrill.

Young Homer's daring behavior amazed the crowd. His antics were starting to make his mother dizzy. She looked behind her to see what was going on, only to discover what Homer was doing. He was snapping back and forth harder than a rubber band from a slingshot! Elsa quickly whirled around, giving Homer a sharp jolt.

"Now listen to me son," she scolded, pointing one of her long blades at Homer. "Do not play tricks on your mother like that again. When I'm flying, you should keep still and just enjoy the ride."

Homer cringed with embarrassment, his face turning bright red.

"You should always mind and listen to what I tell you," Elsa continued. "It's for your own safety, Homer. Do you understand?"

Looking down at all the other helicopters below, Homer nodded, ashamed. He got Elsa's message loud and clear.

The other mothers, taking in the whole scene, were chuckling. Pointing upward toward Homer, they began teasing Elsa. "You have quite the frisky rascal there, Elsa," called out one of the mothers. "We wish you lots of luck raising that wild little 'copter!"

Elsa was embarrassed by the heckling. She vowed to find the best flight instructor for Homer. She knew one day Homer would make her proud.

 # Chapter 2

Homer grew very fast. Soon he was old enough to learn how to fly mothers, fathers, and children on trips through the enormous Grand Canyon. Homer knew right away that he would enjoy his work. His fondest wish was to gracefully soar in the sky, like the birds he often watched gliding freely on the west wind. But first, Homer had to learn how to fly on his own.

The day finally came for Elsa to take Homer to the Whirly Bird Aviation School, in southern Arizona, to meet his flight teacher and pilot, Hank. Elsa strapped Homer tightly on her back, right up against her cabin, and curled the tow-rope securely around him. She wasn't taking any more chances of letting him loose until he was properly trained to fly on his own. Elsa flew her little 'copter piggyback to his new airport.

Hank was a famous instructor who had trained many young helicopters during his career. He didn't allow his students to disobediently romp around the sky. Learning to fly was serious business!

Elsa sternly told Homer, "I want you to always, always listen to Hank. He will not waste valuable time with naughty little 'copters who do not pay attention to his instructions." Then with a big kiss and tight hug, Elsa bid farewell to her son. Homer couldn't see the tears glistening in Elsa's eyes as she turned around and slowly flew away.

With a twinkle in his eye and a slightly crooked smile, Hank walked over to Homer. Hank was tall and skinny, and as he walked, his sandy-brown, rumpled hair blew in the breeze. He was dressed in blue jeans with a wrinkled flight instructor's jacket worn over a frayed T-shirt that peeked out at the neck.

"Hi, ya, pal . . . Nice to meet cha," Hank said, his words forming slowly. "We'll al' have some fun together, and maybe, if we're lucky, we'll find adventure too!"

Homer was so excited to meet his new pilot and hear him say the word "adventure", that when Hank started polishing Homer's blades and checking out each control stick in his cockpit, the little 'copter could hardly stand still.

Looking Homer straight in the eye, Hank said in a friendly tone, "Now listen up, son. I want you to learn the right way that a young helicopter should fly. First, you should fly forward and then climb straight up into the sky as far as you can go." Hank pointed up toward the clouds high overhead. "I want to see if you are fast enough and strong enough to reach those puffy clouds towering above. But, first, Homer, you need to know how each control stick works."

Homer paid close attention as Hank continued, "You have a 'C' stick and a 'P' stick which are located in front of the pilot, and two foot pedals on the floor. When I press the right pedal, you turn right; when I press the left pedal, you turn left. When I push the 'P' stick down, you dive down; when I pull the 'P' stick up, you climb high. When I hold the 'P' stick in the middle, you hover right in midair and keep your blades spinning fast, or we'll drop like a big rock! When I push the 'C' stick forward, you fly straight ahead. When I pull the 'C' stick back, you fly backward."

Hank paused a moment and a grin crossed his face. "Homer, did you know helicopters are the only aircraft that can fly backward? . . . So, got all that?"

Homer's mind began to spin. He wasn't sure he understood all the new instructions.

Hank encouraged his little student, "Now don't worry, Homer. You'll soon get the hang of all your controls working together perfectly."

Hank gave Homer his first tank full of gas. Homer felt a powerful sensation flow throughout his frame. His confidence started to rise but quickly dropped when he began to wonder, "Will my new engine start up right away? Will my blades go 'round and 'round, turning faster and faster, whistling whir . . . whir-r-r-r . . . whir-r-r-r?"

"Now, don't try to do any of those fancy flippy-flops or cartwheels that other new helicopters try," Hank warned, climbing into the pilot's seat. "They only get themselves into a lot of trouble!"

The moment had finally come. Hank turned the start key and pushed on the thrust button. Homer tightly

held his breath then let out a coughing gasp followed by a booming puff of smoke. His engine started up and began making a purring sound. The engine shook louder and louder. Soon it became a deafening roar. Homer's blades began spinning faster and faster. The vibrations felt like a jumbo eggbeater. He was ready to take off. "WHOOPEE!" He shouted.

With a hard, fast jerk, Hank pulled the little 'copter's "P" control stick. This was a brand-new feeling and experience for Homer. He started to wiggle and wobble on his feet. With all his might, Homer gave a giant leapfrog lunge. To his surprise, he lurched straight up into the sky. He began sliding and staggering sideways in a crooked flight pattern -- but at least he was flying! Although Homer had been warned by Hank, he couldn't resist doing at least one big flip-flop followed by a double cartwheel. As he did these fancy tricks, he punched out of the clouds and started falling wildly out of control.

"Help! Oh, help! Somebody help me!" he cried.

Hank quickly corrected Homer's mishap by bringing him back into level flight. "Now listen, Homer, ol' buddy," Hank called out firmly from the pilot's seat. "Ya gotta pay much more attention to your lessons and quit goofing off if you really want to learn to fly. Understand me?"

Homer lowered his eyes. "I'm sorry, Hank," he said guiltily. "From now on, I won't show off any more."

"Good," replied Hank, "then, let's try again." Hank pressed all three of Homer's controls, sending him shooting swiftly back into the air.

Again and again Homer tried and tried his best to fly. At first he flip-flopped by mistake, doing a nosedive toward the ground. Hank quickly yanked the power stick backward. Homer climbed higher and higher, speeding toward the white-capped clouds. But the little 'copter was flying at such a steep angle that his blades stopped spinning. Homer's engine started coughing and all of a sudden quit working. Homer froze dead still, right in midair; he had stalled out!

Homer's whole body turned upside-down, and he slowly floated out of control, going round and round in lazy circles. Spinning in tighter circles, he started to gain speed, coiling into a deadly, tight curve. Again, Hank came to the rescue, pulling Homer into level flight. Soon the little 'copter's crazy flying began to upset Hank's stomach. He

and Homer were getting dizzy.

Hank instructed Homer, "We're both pooped-out. I think we've practiced enough for today. Let's head for home." Hank eased the control sticks to the middle and flew Homer at a gentle pace. Soon they arrived back at the helicopter landing pad. Hank held Homer hovering above the pad while slowly lowering him until his landing skids softly touched the ground.

Homer breathed a sigh of relief as he thought, "It's wonderful to be in the hands of a skilled pilot like Hank. I'll do better next time."

Homer didn't give up. At each lesson he practiced harder, becoming better and better. Then one sunny spring morning, to his utter amazement, Homer found himself flying perfectly. He skillfully circled, spun, and darted sideways, backward, and straight up and down. He even hovered just inches above the ground without flopping over.

Hank was so proud of his new student. Homer had, at last, earned his wings. "Congratulations, Homer," Hank happily hollered, "I knew you could do it!"

Hank then revealed some remarkable news to Homer, "After you have had enough flying experience, you might be able to operate your own controls without a pilot on board. But remember, pilots who fly helicopters have to think and act fast. So you, too, will have to pass the test of patting yourself on the head while rubbing your belly at the same time." Hank teased, "Want to give it a try, Homer?"

Homer decided he'd try that trick another day.

Homer worked hard over the next few months, paying close attention to his lessons. He quickly became very good at flying under Hank's instructions. Hank thought now was the perfect time for Elsa to come for a visit so she could see her little 'copter had become a skillful and obedient flyer. Hank decided Elsa's visit would be a secret; he wanted to surprise Homer! Elsa was thrilled when Hank asked her to fly to the canyon; she promised to meet them the very next day.

 # Chapter 3

Sunrise came early. Hank began polishing Homer's blades and frame; he wanted the little 'copter to be sparkling clean for Elsa.

Homer looked into the sky and was suddenly blinded for a second when he saw what appeared to be a fiery flame fly across the clouds. The golden streak was speeding straight toward him! It made a thundering sound, and Homer quivered, confused and a bit fearful.

When Elsa sped by, Homer breathed a sigh of relief; his fears quickly vanished the minute he recognized what the golden streak was. "It's my mother! It's my mother, Elsa!" Homer wildly yelled to Hank. Hank mischievously winked at the little 'copter and shouted: "Surprise!" Homer was so happy to see his mother he started bouncing up and down in glee like a Pogo stick-- boink . . . boink . . . boink.

Elsa soon landed. She and Homer hugged each other lovingly. Elsa smothered Homer with motherly kisses. Homer scrunched-up his face in embarrassment; Elsa was treating him like the little, childish helicopter he was the day she turned him over to Hank. Homer stood as tall as he could and said, "Mom, I'm not a baby helicopter anymore. Hank has taught me to fly perfectly." Homer smiled, full of pride, showing off his flight wings. "When Hank gave me my flight wings, he said I can steer my own controls without a pilot on board, after I gain more experience."

Elsa was delighted. She was very proud of her son, and grateful to Hank for his patient flight instruction.

Elsa couldn't wait to see her little 'copter fly. "That's wonderful, Homer, congratulations! Let's test your skills to see what you've learned." Before Homer could utter a word, Elsa's powerful blades started spinning and she was instantly airborne. She motioned Homer to join her by himself without Hank on board. Elsa instructed Homer, "Fly behind me and do exactly what I do." She assured her son, "Don't worry. If you get into any trouble, I'll help you."

Then the fun began!

Elsa swiftly whirled around and began flying a precise zigzag pattern. Homer realized he had to watch her carefully, think fast, and stay close, zigzagging in the same direction, just as if he were Elsa's shadow. Zig-zag-zig . . . zag-zig-zag . . . zig-zag-zig . . . , through the sky they raced! The peppy Homer had become so nimble he startled his mother by zigging and zagging only seconds behind her.

Elsa broadly smiled at Homer with approval and signaled him to land. Elsa stayed in the air to teach one more lesson. She steeply tilted her blades sideways and then immediately tilted them in the opposite direction performing a lightning-quick wing-wag-wave without stalling out. Then, barely inches above the ground Elsa snapped into level flight. She hovered downward and gently landed right in front of Homer. Hank and Homer had never seen such expert flying! Homer knew he'd need more training before he could attempt such a daring stunt.

Homer hugged his mother and told her, "You're the greatest, mom!"

Tears of joy filled Elsa's eyes; she said, "I'm very proud of you, Homer! You've grown from being a disobedient little 'copter into a skillful flyer. Those mother helicopters who teased us will be surprised when I tell them about your progress!"

The sun was sinking low in the horizon. It was time for Elsa to depart. Before lifting off, Elsa said, "Homer, you're almost a full-fledged helicopter. Hank has taught you well, and you're lucky he's your pilot. I wish you and Hank fair weather flying!" Homer and Elsa embraced each other one last time.

Homer and Hank watched Elsa fly westward. Her brilliant strobe lights flashed through the night sky as she swiftly disappeared.

 # Chapter 4

The next morning dawned bright and sunny. Hank started Homer's engine and pointed the 'copter's nose in the direction of the Grand Canyon, located in Arizona's desert. After flying over the vast desert, Homer was first to spot the massive canyon. His blades shuddered as he stared in awe and disbelief.

The intense sun lit up the many thousands of rocks on the canyon's surface, making them glitter like enormous jewels. There were colors of purple, green, red, blue, brown, yellow, orange, and pink, all mixed together like shades of the rainbow. Homer had never seen anything so splendid in all his life. There were finger-like cliffs, which jutted straight up out of the bottom and climbed an entire mile to the top rim. As Homer and Hank flew closer to the rocky spires, Homer became uneasy. The jagged cliffs looked as if they might reach out and snatch him right out of the sky! Homer's mind raced, "I must respect these dangerous cliffs," he told himself. "I'll fly around them carefully and keep my eyes on where I'm going so that I don't give the treacherous rocks a chance to grab me. Hank trusts my flying and I don't want to disappointment him."

Hank and Homer were now ready to begin their new job as aerial tour guides. The passengers would be taking lots of pictures of the canyon's beautiful scenery, its swift river, and deep gorge. It would be Homer's job to circle around the sharp cliffs, then fly through the bottom of the canyon in a tight, figure-eight pattern, just a few feet above the dangerous river. The fast water wildly rushed over slick rocks, churning itself into rapids that made a roaring, hissing noise like an erupting volcano. The powerful river practically boiled over its banks.

Under Hank's expert guidance, Homer flew many trips through the canyon. Step-by-step he learned to operate his own controls without Hank's assistance. Homer practiced tilting his blades and sharply turning to avoid hitting any cliffs. The little 'copter soon became such a skilled flyer that he could easily steer through any part of the canyon as he came to know the great cliffs, valleys, rocks, rims, trees, river, and landmarks. Hank was proud of Homer and his performance flying solo. Hank still felt he needed to keep a watchful eye on the frisky little 'copter, though, just in case . . .

One day, while practicing flying drills near the bottom of the canyon, Homer finally gathered up enough courage to introduce himself to the river. "Hi! My name is Homer. What's yours?"

The river, with a giant GURR-R-R-R, roared its warning, "My name is The Colorado! I am the longest, fastest, and most famous river in the West! They call me 'The Mighty Water'. It took me a million years, but my power carved out this vast canyon. I would never try to land in me if I were you! You'd probably drown!"

Homer shivered at the thought of such an event ever happening to him and Hank. Homer made a hasty retreat. He climbed straight up and popped over the canyon's rim at a high rate of speed!

As time went by, Homer became even better at flying through the huge canyon. He loved his new job, especially meeting all the children who would come aboard. He cradled them safely inside his strong frame, always protecting them. Sometimes Homer gave the children a special treat by taking them on one of his rare, daring flights. Steeply plunging down into the rugged canyon, he frolicked and skipped along between the sheer cliffs, barely dodging them, making the boys' and girls' stomachs turn upside down!

The children cheered and giggled with delight. They'd plead with Homer, "Do it again, do it again! Please, please, please, Homer, do it again!" But Homer was very cautious and mindful of those little ones in his care, so he wisely told them, "Sorry, kids, but that's the end of your dizzy joy ride for today." Homer then delivered the tired children into the arms of their parents, bidding each boy and girl a warm good night.

The children loved flying around the canyon with Homer. They promptly nicknamed him, The Cliffhangin' Helicopter.

Before going to sleep at night, Homer and Hank watched the bright moonlight shine on the jagged rocks. Craggy shadows crawled across the valley, stretching into eerie-shaped forms that looked as if they wanted to eat Homer and Hank! The two friends chuckled at the weird grimaces the shadows seemed to make. Then Homer drifted off to dreamland, thinking, "I'm so lucky! I get to fly around the Grand Canyon, one of nature's Seven Wonders of the World."

 # Chapter 5

One morning, Hank was flying Homer to a brand-new airport on the other side of the Grand Canyon. This would be Homer's new home. Homer didn't have much to keep him busy on this flight as there were no passengers on board. So he flew along, gazing lazily at the passing scenery and the billowing clouds.

He was suddenly jolted when an enormous bird soared right over the top of his blades! The creature's head was covered with snow-white feathers. His thick, brownish-black wing feathers rustled in the breeze. The bird's piercing eyes, which could see for miles, darted back and forth, and his sharp talons curled around the bottom of his powerful, yellow feet. The bird's hooked beak glistened in the sunlight, and his long, strong wings flapped as he searched the ground beneath for any sign of food.

Homer couldn't believe his eyes. The magnificent bird was none other than a bald eagle (our own noble American symbol). It was the first eagle the little 'copter had ever seen.

The eagle instantly caught sight of Homer. Startled, Homer tried his best to dodge the huge creature. Circling around in a split second, the mighty bird swooped down and screeched at the top of his lungs, "Get out of my canyon and my domain! This is my territory!" With eyes blazing and talons fully extended, the daring bird prepared to attack Homer head-on. Speeding straight toward Homer, the eagle's razor-like talons struck the little 'copter's head, hitting his windshield and almost knocking him out of the sky, giving Homer several nasty cuts on his forehead and cheek. He lurched down rapidly toward the canyon's deep crevices.

Hank was caught off guard, but he swiftly grabbed the little 'copter's controls and brought him back into level flight. "Hey, ol' buddy," Hank shouted above the uproar. "We better not trespass into that bird's territory. Let's get out'a here as fast as we can!"

Although Homer had promised to obey Hank, he was so upset he couldn't follow Hank's orders. The eagle had

made him so mad! "Besides," Homer thought, "I want to show that darned bird I'm not afraid of him! I'm just as brave and skillful as he is. He's just a big bully!" But, deep down, Homer envied the powerful eagle's boldness and strength.

Homer wanted to learn more about the eagle, but didn't want to get cut again, so decided he'd try to be friendly. Doing his best not to quiver, Homer approached the strong bird. As soon as he was close enough, he spoke, "Hello . . . It's me again. My name is . . . um, Homer. I'm a quick, silver helicopter. What's your name, sir?"

The eagle never expected that such a laughable helicopter would dare venture back into his sky. The proud bird simply glared at Homer. He was curious about a small flying machine that made its blades swirl around in a whirring noise and burned smelly gasoline simply to stay in the air. The eagle squinted his eyes, stretched open his beak, and boasted, "I am Mr. Baldazar, descendant of the Russian Eagle Czars, the rulers of olden times. I control the skies over this entire canyon. In fact, they call me the 'The Thunderbolt of the Sky'. I'm the grandest bird in all the land!"

The eagle continued to brag, "My mighty call is heard throughout this great canyon! Schre-e-e-e-ch! Schre-e-e-e-ch!" Baldazar's voice pierced the air with strong vibrations; the force even blasted some paint right off Homer's nose. The little 'copter was startled to see the silver paint specs whiz past his eyes.

"And furthermore," Baldazar bellowed, "I can fly circles around you, Homer!" The eagle tucked his wings tightly against his body and did an upside-down split-S turn away from Homer and, like a speeding bullet, then dove down headfirst toward the Colorado River.

Homer was so amazed at the eagle's spectacular flying that for a moment he forgot that he was just a little 'copter. He wanted to chase Baldazar and do the same tricks. So Homer slowed down his blades just enough to keep himself in the air and dove steeply toward the deep gorge, trying all the way down to catch Baldazar.

All of a sudden, before Hank could pull Homer out of his dive, the little 'copter lost control, barely skimming across the mighty Colorado River. The river's stern warning, never to land in it, flashed across his mind. Homer was so low that his landing skids became completely drenched in the rough water. With a loud clunk, he slammed into the huge rocks. Thud! . . . Ka-boom! . . . Bang! The massive boulders clattered and rattled all over the shore. Jagged splinters of rock tore large holes in the little 'copter's shiny body, tossing and scattering his parts all about. Homer

21

had CRASHED! One sharp fragment flew up and sliced the top of his nose, leaving a scar.

Just before Homer had lost control, Hank had tightly buckled himself inside the 'copter's frame, hoping to ride-out the crash and not get thrown onto the spiked rocks. Hank held on with all his might. He was bruised and torn-up with scratches, but luckily he wasn't badly injured like Homer. Hank was shaken-up from head to toe; he'd never been in such a horrible crash!

Thudd-d-d! . . . Ka-boom-m-m! . . . Bang-g-g! . . . . Rip-p-p! Suddenly the noises of Homer's dreadful wreck bounced back and forth, echoing off the canyon's high, sheer cliffs.

Homer was stunned and in pain, but worse, he could hardly believe he'd actually taken the controls away from Hank, his pilot, causing their crash. Homer felt terrible. He knew he should have obeyed Hank's commands, but now it was too late.

Hank was very upset with Homer's actions. He never thought such a well-trained helicopter would suffer such a crushing accident. The frown on Hank's face reflected his disappointment, but he didn't scold Homer. Hank could see the little 'copter was ashamed of his reckless flying. Homer needed Hank's help more than ever now.

When Baldazar saw Homer and Hank crash, feelings of sorrow and regret swept over the eagle. He had never meant to seriously injure the little 'copter. Baldazar swiftly flew over to the banged-up pair and started comforting them by stroking his soft feathery wings all around torn Homer and bruised Hank. Baldazar humbly pleaded, "Homer, please forgive my awfully bad behavior and my scratching your windshield. I was only trying to protect my canyon home and got carried away. I'm truly sorry. Oh... and to think that I started the whole thing!"

Homer's mouth dropped open in disbelief. This stubborn eagle was apologizing and trying to soothe his and Hank's pain. Homer thought, "Amazing! Baldazar isn't just tough, he has a caring heart as well."

Baldazar's head drooped and he admitted, "To tell the truth, Homer, I've been so lonely in this canyon all by myself, with no friends, that I really just wanted to play. In fact, I was going to teach you how to soar just like me. Think of the fun we could have flying around together!"

Homer and Hank softened toward the eagle. Homer replied, "Don't feel bad, Baldazar. We're very happy that you want to be our friend and help us." Hank nodded in agreement.

Homer spoke up again, "I'd love to learn to soar like an eagle, Baldazar, and explore the canyon with you, but right now we've got to figure out how to reach someone who'll come and rescue us from this disaster." Homer sadly looked up at his bent blades and sighed, "I'll never fly again unless I can get to the helicopter factory for repairs."

Baldazar moved closer to Hank and Homer. He would guard the injured twosome until someone came to their rescue.

Hank and Homer realized they were in a terrible mess. Who would ever find them at the bottom of this gigantic canyon?

 # Chapter 6

The sun was beginning to set, and the dark chilly night would soon be upon them. Baldazar began scratching the top of his feathery white head, trying to come up with an idea that might help Homer and Hank. He wanted to make up for treating his new friends so cruelly. Baldazar knew he had to take some kind of action before it was too late. Suddenly the eagle's intense eyes lit up. He had the perfect idea! "Listen, you two," he said to Homer and Hank. "I'm going to fly to the nearby army base and bring back some soldiers to rescue you. My journey will take about two hours, but don't worry, I'll be back as fast as I can fly."

With deep sighs of relief, both Hank and Homer gave Baldazar a smile as they wished him good luck. Baldazar flapped his wings with such great force that he bolted straight up and disappeared over the canyon's highest rim. To prevent getting lost, the clever eagle set his sights on the brilliantly flickering North Star; it would guide him back and forth through the dark moonless sky.

The accident had left Hank bruised and sore, but he stayed close by Homer's side caring for him as best he could. Hank needed a good night's sleep to regain his energy and all the strength he could muster to perform the risky task of tightly bracing Homer into a rope harness so the soldiers could lift the 'copter out of the canyon.

Baldazar bravely rushed to the army base, flying as fast as he could. The minute he spotted soldiers, the tired eagle landed and told them about the crash. A crew of three soldiers promised they'd start out at the crack of dawn to rescue the downed pair. Baldazar then hastily flew back to the canyon and delivered the soldiers' message to his extremely cold and weary friends.

The black midnight sky soon surrounded the three. Baldazar perched himself on top of Homer's blades. He kept Hank and Homer warm, all through the night, by cloaking them in his enormous, thick wings. To Homer and Hank, it was unbelievable to see Baldazar acting like a fussy mother hen, but both were very grateful. The eagle truly had a caring heart after all.

The warmth from Baldazar's wings comforted Hank. His bruises and scratches began to heal, and his strength started to return.

The next morning the soldiers arrived for the rescue attempt. They were flying their large yellow Sky Crane chopper, which looked and sounded like a gigantic, buzzing bumblebee. Hank tied a strong rope securely around Homer and then signaled to the soldiers hovering above to hoist his little 'copter up underneath their Sky Crane. Homer would have to dangle about in the open air, swinging and swaying, back and forth, while the soldiers carried him out of the steep canyon.

Hank told Homer, "I'm going back to the Whirly Bird Aviation School to train young 'copters again. You've learned a painful lesson, Homer, but I'm sure you won't be reckless and crash again. I'll miss you very much, but I know we'll see each other again someday, so this isn't goodbye, just, see ya' later ol' pal." Hank smartly saluted Homer, turned and also saluted the soldiers. Hank's deed heartened the little 'copter, and a grin spread across his battered face.

"Okay, men," Hank instructed, "fly as quickly and safely as you can, and get my Homer to the Helicopter Hospital so that he can be repaired right away."

Baldazar couldn't accompany Homer. The eagle had to stay in the Grand Canyon to guide Hank to the Phantom Ranch House. It lay in the very bottom near the river. There the ranch hands could bandage and treat Hank's injuries. As soon as Hank healed, he'd be able to ride one of the ranch's mules up the canyon's steep trail to the top.

Hank and Baldazar waved goodbye to their little buddy. Homer's eyes became misty and he started to cry. Big teardrops slowly dripped down his cheeks. The little 'copter waved back, not really knowing if he'd ever see them again.

❧❧

Angry black clouds rumbled in the West as a wild storm rapidly approached. Thunder clapped sharply, shattering the sky and everything in it. Rough winds tossed Homer all about. Heavy rains pounded down hard on him and the Sky Crane until they were both completely soaked. Zorch! . . . Crackle! . . .Snap! A giant bolt of lightning raced out of the clouds, striking Homer's tail, causing his eyes to nearly pop out of his head! He'd been sky-scorched! Now the little 'copter was not only wrecked but his tail was burned coal black! Little did he know he wasn't out of trouble yet.

When the lightning hit Homer it also charred the bottom of the army helicopter, but it was made of strong, sturdy rubber-padded metal so the soldiers didn't get hurt. They had never flown a rescue mission through such a dangerous storm and were anxious to reach the end of this journey!

The army chopper soon arrived at the Helicopter Hospital. The soldiers spotted the area where young helicopters and airplanes were being fixed. Homer was dropped with a loud splash right into a mud puddle in the back row with other broken aircraft. The army Sky Crane was glad to get rid of him!

The minute all the shiny, repaired airplanes and helicopters spotted Homer, they pointed at him and laughed, "Why, just take a look at that ridiculous, sky-scorched thing!" one teased. "Who let him in here?" The jokes made Homer feel even worse than he had before. He wanted nothing more than to be fixed so that he could fly once again. Then the other aircraft couldn't poke fun at him anymore.

With a mournful, low sigh, Homer waited outside for his turn to be towed into the Helicopter Hospital and fixed. But the repairmen were so busy working on other helicopters that they never came to fetch him. It was right then and there that Homer promised himself again, and made a silent promise to Hank, that for the rest of his life he would be the most well-behaved and careful 'copter ever!

Soon the icy winter wind and cold snow came blowing across the Arizona high country. When spring finally arrived, Homer could smell the blossoms of the sweet flowers. This made him feel a little better. He still patiently waited, but was beginning to believe he might never be repaired and have to live the rest of his life in the junk heap.

 # Chapter 7

One sunny morning, Homer was gazing down his line of parked helicopters when he smelled perfume. "What a strange smell to be in a place like this," he thought. Homer squinted, looking harder, and soon the prettiest woman he had ever seen walked around the corner. She had lovely turquoise eyes shadowed by long black lashes. The brisk breeze blew her short, dark hair about her face. The young lady was neatly dressed in a crisp white flight suit and a glossy, silver-trimmed jacket. Pinned all over her jacket were shiny medals she'd been awarded for her flying achievements while piloting helicopters and airplanes.

The young woman's name was Jennie. She was checking each helicopter carefully as she needed to find just the right one to help her in a new job. Out of the corner of her eye, Jennie spotted Homer and then glanced over toward him, surprised at what she saw. Even though his tail was out of shape and burned black, Homer stretched out his bent blades and straightened up his crooked frame as tall as he could. Then he winked one beaming eye at Jennie while smiling his widest, brightest grin. When Jennie saw Homer's round face, dancing eyes, and efforts to attract her attention, she couldn't help but admire this special little helicopter. She was hooked on Homer at once!

Walking over to Homer, Jennie reached out and stroked his broken frame. She gave the little 'copter a hug to let him know she was very happy to find him. Then Jennie exclaimed, "I've been searching and searching and finally found you. You are the perfect 'copter for me to fly on our new medical search and rescue missions." Jennie's voice was as pretty as she was.

"I am Jennie. What's your name?"

"Homer." He answered, still grinning.

Homer couldn't help comparing Jennie and Hank. "Jennie is so beautiful and completely opposite of ol' Hank," he thought.

Jennie questioned Homer, "What happened to you? How did you get so badly bent and ripped?"

Homer told Jennie the whole story of his adventures with Hank and their encounter with Baldazar in the Grand Canyon.

The little 'copter briefly related the events of his crash to Jennie, how he wanted to impress Baldazar and lost control, his wreck in the Colorado River, and the eagle's kindness as he flew to the army base for help. Homer told Jennie about the soldiers flying their Sky Crane to the canyon, and transporting him through the ferocious thunderstorm to the factory hospital.

As Homer finished, he breathed a sigh, looking up at Jennie. "Jennie, I've learned my lesson and don't want to ever crash again . . . Never another accident!"

Jennie was relieved to hear his pledge. She replied, "It sounds like you've experienced quite a bit of adventure, Homer! I'm glad these flying lessons have turned you into a wiser helicopter."

Jennie continued, "Well then, Homer, we'll be going on risky flights in the wilderness and forests surrounding the Grand Canyon. Our mission will be searching the rugged territory for ranch homes where injured and ill children will be awaiting medical help. My job will be loading the children onto your stretcher, Homer."

Jennie smiled at Homer, giving him a pat on the nose. "Your job will be to quickly and safely fly the children to large city hospitals, where the doctors and nurses can treat each child. They'll all be depending on us, so I'm glad you know every twist and turn in the canyon."

Jennie informed Homer, "I'm going to make you into the smallest Air Ambulance Medical 'copter in the country. But you'll have to practice very hard learning to land on top of the hospital's heliport, which is on the building's sheer, windy ledge."

Homer was overjoyed that he was going to have permission to land on the heliport just like the big medical helicopters. Now he could prove to the others that he was an ace flyer and not just some piece of junk. Homer giggled as he thought, "Those helicopters that teased me won't be able to poke fun at me again!"

31

"Oh, thank you, Jennie!" Homer told her gratefully. "It'll be my pleasure to help you and the children."

Upon Jennie's orders, the repairmen promptly moved Homer into the helicopter's operating room. They hammered away on his metal skin and blades, and welded on new parts, patching up his ugly holes and cuts. Jennie told the repair crew to add an extra blade on top of Homer to give him more speed and control. This would make him the fastest medical helicopter in the fleet! Soon Homer's three blades, skin, and tail were completely straight once more.

Jennie was eager to start flying her little 'copter, so the painters decided to hurry and finish his repairs. Rather than using paintbrushes, they grabbed Homer, dragged him over to a fat barrel of glittering, diamond-silver paint, and dunked him in headfirst! Homer had just enough time to tightly close his eyes and hold his breath as he went under. He came up dripping wet and

gasping for air, but grinning from ear to ear. He glittered brighter than a brand-new silver coin! Homer looked quite different from before. The paint had created several dazzling silver streaks running the length of his body to the end of his tail, giving him a modern, sleek appearance. At last, Homer was all fixed up and ready to go.

When Jennie saw her little 'copter sparkling and looking so handsome, she hollered, "Wow!" and jumped into his new pilot's seat. Jennie started Homer's engine, and pulled the power stick all the way up. Homer's sharp new blades began spinning very fast, then faster and faster as they powerfully sliced through the cool evening air. With a loud shout, Homer bolted straight up into the crystal clear sky, "Hurrah!" He climbed higher and higher, through the puffy clouds.

"Leaping lizards!" he yelled with excitement. Homer, the Grand Canyon quick-silver-streak 'copter was, at last, flying once again.

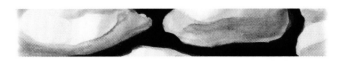 # Chapter 8

Jennie then told Homer, "Before we begin your training I'd like to meet your mother, Elsa and get her approval to pilot you as an Air Ambulance Medical chopper. I want her to see you've grown into a responsible helicopter."

Jennie shot Homer a grin. "I also think Elsa will be surprised how handsome you look now."

Homer heartily agreed, "Great! I'd love to visit my mother. She and the other mothers will be amazed when they see my new sleek paint and powerful third blade."

Jennie and Homer began their flight to the helicopter factory where he was born. When the two arrived, they saw Elsa below chatting with the other helicopters. "Let's approach quietly from behind and then fly fast overhead, revving up my engine into a roaring noise to see if they recognize me," Homer excitedly suggested to Jennie.

Jennie thought about Homer's suggestion for a few moments. "Well, . . . I don't know if that's such a good idea," Homer. "Oh, okay, . . . Just this once. I just hope we don't frighten Elsa and upset her."

The mischievous 'copter replied, "I'll take that chance. This is probably the only time I may be able to catch my mother off-guard!"

Jennie pulled Homer's power stick back to dim the sound of his engine and then pushed the controls all the way forward. Homer thundered through the air! He and Jennie zoomed by Elsa at a high rate of speed. Elsa and the others were shocked to see a silver-streaked helicopter fly by at such a daring pace. Homer's diamond paint dazzled their eyes. Elsa didn't recognize her son. Jennie tilted the little 'copter's blades sideways, turned around, and the two of them slowly flew back. Elsa was stunned to see the nimble helicopter was none other than her own Homer, and that a pretty lady was sitting in his pilot's seat. Elsa was puzzled, "What has happened to my Homer, who is this person flying him, and where is Hank?"

Jennie and Homer soon landed. Elsa strode over to Homer, scooped him up, and in a brisk voice said, "Young man don't startle your mother like that ever again!" But Elsa couldn't hide her excitement to see her son once more. She warmly smiled, winked and gave him a big hug. Homer lovingly hugged her back and explained, "I wanted to fly rapidly by and surprise you with my power, speed, and new 'look'. Oh, . . . I'm so happy to see you, mom!"

Homer then politely introduced Elsa and Jennie to each other and eagerly added, "Mom, Jennie is the best lady pilot in the West! She's an ace flyer." Elsa was glad to meet Jennie and learn Homer was in the hands of an expert pilot. Jennie was very happy she'd finally met Homer's mother.

Elsa examined Homer, looking him up and down and all over. She raised her eyebrows in concern as she questioned, "Homer, why do you have such flashy stripes and a third blade now? What happened to you?"

Jennie and Homer told Elsa all the adventures and mishaps the little 'copter had experienced. They related how Hank and Homer had worked as tour guides in the Grand Canyon and grown to love the tourist children. They described the little 'copter's meeting Baldazar and explained why Homer had crashed.

Elsa was distressed by Homer's story. "But what happened to Hank? Where is he now, and why is Jennie your new pilot?" Elsa asked him.

"Hank got bruised and scratched in the crash, but, thankfully, he wasn't seriously injured. He went back to the Whirly Bird Aviation School to train young helicopters again." Homer replied.

Homer went on to tell his mother of how he met Jennie, and Jennie explained Homer's new job.

Elsa was grateful Jennie had found Homer and had him repaired, but more so, she was delighted her son was going to become an Air Ambulance Medical chopper.

The other mothers spoke up congratulating Elsa on her son's accomplishments. Elsa beamed. She was very proud of Homer too.

Even though Jennie, Homer and Elsa's visit continued long into the night, the next morning came too quickly, and it was time for Homer and Jennie to leave.

Elsa warmly smiled at Jennie and said, "Thank you for helping Homer! I know you will make him into a proficient Air Ambulance helicopter. It was nice to meet you, Jennie, and I'm sure we'll meet again someday. Here's wishing you and Homer fair weather flying."

Elsa turned to Homer. "You were lucky to meet Jennie. I want you to obey her instructions and train hard for your medical missions." Elsa curved one of her long blades around Homer wrapping him tightly. "Make me proud, son!" As the little 'copter and Elsa hugged each other goodbye she whispered, "Oh . . . Yes, Homer, . . . be sure to keep your promise, and never crash again."

Elsa watched Jennie and Homer fly toward the Grand Canyon. Homer's silver streaks flashed through the blue sky. Elsa's eyes shimmered with tears. She sighed as she thought, "It seems like only yesterday when I turned my son over to Hank for his first flying lessons. Homer's no longer my little 'copter. He's matured into a talented and powerful flyer."

 # Chapter 9

Homer quickly completed his training as an Air Ambulance helicopter, and started his new job, with Jennie expertly piloting him through the Grand Canyon's vast wilderness. During rescue flights Homer carefully transported each child inside his soft, strong cabin, making the boys and girls feel safe and secure on their long journey.

One crisp autumn morning Homer and Jennie set off to pick up a very sick boy named Michael who lived on a farm at the edge of the canyon. As they neared the high, mountainous rim, Homer's thoughts turned to Baldazar. He wondered if the eagle still lived in the canyon's golden-colored cliffs. Three years had passed since the day they'd said their good-byes after Homer's crash. While flying toward their destination, Homer searched the sky for Baldazar, but the morning rapidly passed with no sign of his friend.

When they arrived at the farmhouse, Jennie and Michael's father quickly loaded the little lad onto the stretcher, carried him over to Homer, and buckled him securely into one of the cabin seats. Jennie gave Michael some medicine that the doctors had sent along so that he'd be able to survive the flight comfortably.

Although Homer wished he could go looking for Baldazar, he knew that getting Michael to the hospital as soon as possible was more important. Homer started his engine running at full speed, forcing his blades to go round and round. He then lunged upward and was instantly airborne.

As he looked up, the sun's rays reflected off a pair of sharp, glistening talons. Blinding light flashed across Homer's startled eyes as he caught a glimpse of an eagle's huge black wings soaring out of the white clouds.

"Could it be? . . . It must be? . . . It had to be . . . Baldazar!" Homer wildly imagined. But his heart quickly sank as he saw the big bird turn away and head toward the opposite end of the canyon. He asked Jennie if they could fly after the eagle, just for a minute, to see if it really was his friend. When Jennie saw Homer's hopeful eyes gazing back at her, it was hard to resist his request. Glancing over at Michael, Jennie saw some color had returned to his

cheeks. Jennie thought, "The medicine must be working . . . A few minutes detouring will be all right." So Jennie granted the little 'copter permission. "Okay, Homer, but only just for a moment. I, too, would very much like to find Baldazar and meet him." Homer had told Jennie all about the first time he'd met Baldazar and how he'd tried but couldn't match the eagle's incredible flying skills.

Homer decided to attract Baldazar's attention by pulling a prank on his eagle friend. So Homer revved-up his engine until it grew into a thunderous, roaring noise, which caused his blades to shatter the air with the shrillest sound they'd ever made. Upon hearing such an awful racket, the eagle's ears perked straight up. He couldn't imagine who was making this loud uproar, giving him such a terrible jolt and disturbing his peace.

The mighty bird banked his wings into a steep turn, soaring closer and closer to the noise. Soon Homer and Baldazar came face to face. Homer was so overcome with joy at finally finding Baldazar that he cried out, "Oh . . . YIPPEE! . . . I can't believe it. Thank goodness I found you at last, Baldazar!"

Baldazar gleefully screeched back, "I don't believe it, either . . . It is really you, my long-lost friend Homer! HURRAH!" Taking another look at Homer, Baldazar remarked, "Whoa-a-a . . . Do I believe what I'm seeing? . . . A striped, silver-streaked 'copter? Why, I could draw lines down your side and use you to play tick-tack-toe!" The two friends' laughter filled the air with merriment.

Baldazar and Homer hugged each other tightly. In their gaiety neither one of them noticed that a large silver paint spot had rubbed off onto the eagle's white tail feathers and a smaller spot had coated one of his wing tips.

The two happy pals frolicked through autumn's purple-blue sky, circling, spinning, and chasing each other as they used to do. The clever Baldazar, still up to his old flying tricks, steeply dived down right over the top of Homer and Jennie's heads. But Homer, remembering his awful crash in the canyon, his promise not to show off again and especially since little Michael was onboard, didn't try to match the eagle's advanced flying stunts.

When Homer and Baldazar stopped long enough to catch their breath, the little 'copter realized that, by mistake, he'd taken the controls away from Jennie for several minutes. Jennie didn't scold him this time and simply relaxed, enjoying the ride. Finally, remembering his manners, Homer introduced her to Baldazar.

Jennie couldn't resist the urge to tease them. "Although you two have just taken me on a wild ride and broken every rule in the Safe Flight Manual, I'm delighted to meet you at last, Mr. Baldazar. You are exactly as daring and as playful as Homer described." Jennie tossed Baldazar a kiss. He was so embarrassed that for the first time in his life the stalwart eagle blushed.

Suddenly, Baldazar noticed the spots of silver paint sparkling off his tail and wing tip. He realized the paint had rubbed off when he'd hugged Homer. Baldazar flapped his wings and shook his feathers as hard as he could, trying to loosen the paint. He even attempted to strip the paint off by cleaning his feathers with his strong beak, but no matter how hard he tried, the paint stuck fast.

"Darn you, Homer," Baldazar pouted, "see what you've done? Now, how am I going to sneak down upon my prey to catch them? They'll spot me coming a mile away!"

Homer thought this was hilarious. He teased his friend, "Now you glitter just like I do! You could try flying under a passing rain cloud and let the downpour wash the paint off, but you'd get as soaked as a wet dish rag, feathers and all!" The idea of a wet and limp Baldazar threw Homer into fits of laughter. Baldazar didn't find anything funny about this whatsoever.

The minutes had flown by quickly. Jennie was keeping a close eye on Michael, making sure he was okay, but the lad's medicine was beginning to wear off. Homer and Jennie had to get Michael to the hospital right away.

Forgetting his troubles for the time being, Baldazar announced, "I'll guide you two out of this treacherous canyon and painted wilderness and will be your guide whenever you return." Of course, the haughty eagle couldn't help adding, "Whether you want me to or not!" Jennie and Homer were only too happy to accept Baldazar's assistance.

While the three had been enjoying each other's company, they'd failed to notice that a sandstorm was forming in the distant desert sky.

 # Chapter 10

It was still a long way to the hospital. The three travelers picked up the pace to make up for lost time. The air seemed eerily still for a time, but eventually the wind started to pick up a bit, ruffling Baldazar's feathers, and making the ride a bit bumpy for Michael and Jennie. Homer compensated as best he could for the turbulent wind.

Suddenly, the wind became violent and started to shriek. All at once, the looming sandstorm rolled over the threesome, surrounding them on all sides. Not only were their lives in danger, but so was little Michael's!

The storm pounded on, flipping them about like helpless match-sticks. The wind howled and twisted at lightning speed. It created mean dust devils, -- swirling dust and sand that made it hard to see. The dust devils tried to gobble up Homer, Jennie and Baldazar at every turn.

They tried to flee, but were thrown right into the center of the winds and brutally tossed about. Their situation became worse with each passing minute; soon the three friends couldn't see anything through the blinding sand and grit, making it impossible to escape.

Michael was becoming ill again. His face turned a sickly green color, and he began to moan. Jennie wanted to take care of Michael, but the storm's wicked turbulence shook Homer's frame so forcefully Jennie's seat belt popped loose. She bounced wildly from one side of Homer's cabin to the other. Just as Jennie reached down to tighten her seat belt, her forehead hit the window hard. BAM! The impact knocked Jennie unconscious. Homer and Baldazar gasped in shock. They knew that they could crash at any moment if something wasn't done right away.

It seemed like hours, though only a few minutes had passed when Jennie regained consciousness, to Homer and Baldazar's relief. Although dizzy, she was still able to pilot Homer. Jennie gathered up all her courage and seized the controls. Homer's engine was clogged with gritty sand. He started to cough and wheeze. The only thing Jennie and Homer could see, through the twisting sand, was the bright paint smeared all over Baldazar's tail feathers and wing tips, which flashed like sparkling diamonds.

Of course! The perfect idea struck Homer. He called out to Jennie, "Let's use Baldazar's tail like a beacon and follow him to the hospital! After all, that eagle's always bragging how great a guide he is, so now is the time for him to prove it, right, Jennie?"

"You bet. Let's try!" Jennie hollered back.

With that, Homer practically shrieked over the roaring wind, "Hey, you up front, there, Baldazar!" The eagle swiftly circled around. Homer yelled, "All we can see are your glittering feathers through this blowing sand, Baldazar. You claim to know every crag and crevice of this desolate desert. Do you think you can lead us out of here?"

The proud eagle shouted back, "You bet I can! I can spot every rock, hill, and valley in this territory. It's been my hunting ground for years. We'll have to fly very low, though, in order to stay together. This is risky but it's our only hope."

Baldazar flipped around and bolted up right in front of Jennie and Homer. The eagle bellowed to them, "Keep your eyes on me and repeat every move I make. Stay right on my tail; I'm your wing man!"

Each of the three took a deep breath. Against all odds, the trio fiercely fought through the savage storm. Sandy grit beat hard against Baldazar's beak as he flew into the forceful gusts. The eagle's splendid beak quickly became scarred.

Homer's prior experiences of dodging the rugged cliffs in the Grand Canyon came in handy. Homer, Jennie, and Baldazar flew so close to the hills they could feel the scorching desert heat from the rocks below. To make matters worse, all of Homer's parts were so clogged by dirt and sand that he barely limped along. He was in danger of stalling out at any minute and falling to the ground. Jennie rapidly switched each of Homer's controls back and forth and back and forth again, to shake out the sand and keep him in the air.

The three friends plodded on in a zigzag pattern, trying to avoid the cruel dust devils. To keep calm, Homer turned his thoughts back to his childhood memories, remembering fondly his first flight behind his mother and how he'd made her dizzy by zigging when she zagged. If Elsa were here, she'd destroy these dust devils with one swipe

of her forceful blades! Oh, how he missed her.

Michael was dreadfully ill. His face changed from green to ash white. The little lad was clinging to life.

Suddenly, the nasty storm whirled around in the opposite direction. The swirling winds wrapped up the three into one big rolling heap and spit them out! Their stinging eyes drank in the sunshine. Baldazar, Jennie, and Homer found themselves hurtling toward the hospital at a swift speed. The hospital was now only minutes away!

The sight of the hospital was certainly welcome, but the three friends weren't out of trouble yet.

Chapter 11

Homer's controls were so jammed that he shook violently and couldn't maintain power any longer. His blades finally stalled out, and he rapidly lost control thirty feet above the hospital roof's landing pad. Jennie desperately wanted to prevent what would surely be a hard fall for Homer, but there was nothing she could do.

Thud! Homer hit the roof with a jarring jolt. He instantly bounced back into the air and then crashed down again. Crunch! His metal skids kicked up sparks as he slid across the concrete slab, screeching every inch of the way. He came to a blazing stop, just inches from the roof's edge. Luckily, though, since the repairmen had done such a fine job of molding Homer into a sturdy Air Ambulance, neither the little 'copter, Jennie, nor Michael were injured.

As the larger ambulance helicopters watched Homer's landing, they couldn't help but recognize courage in one of their own. They gasped and then cheered as the little 'copter came to a stop. "Bravo, Homer, bravo! You're the new hero of our helicopter fleet!"

Baldazar was absolutely exhausted. His wings sagged, and he fell out of the sky, plopping down with an awful splatter next to Homer. Whoosh! Splat! Feathers went flying everywhere! Baldazar looked more like a half-plucked chicken than a noble eagle.

Doctors and nurses ran out onto the heliport, loaded Michael and Jennie onto stretchers, and rushed them to the emergency room. The medical teams started treating Michael immediately. They gave him large spoonfuls of strong medicine and wrapped him in damp, warm blankets. The nurses gently rubbed the lad's face, arms and legs. Gradually, the color returned to Michael's cheeks, and he was finally out of danger.

Jennie's wounds were quickly cleaned and stitched, and a large bandage was placed over the injury on her forehead.

Baldazar was taken to the animal hospital where doctors patched up his beak and mended his torn feathers. In the morning the eagle would be airlifted to his nest in the high cliffs of the canyon. This was the perfect spot for him to rest and heal.

In the meantime, Homer had been hauled off to the same hospital where he was first repaired on the day Jennie found him. This time, the workmen promptly patched up the little 'copter. After molding him back into shape, they whispered to each other, "Shall we dunk Homer into the barrel of silver paint again?" The men sneaked up behind Homer, grabbed him, and dragged him over to the paint barrel.

"Yikes!" yelped Homer, realizing what was about to happen. In he went, head first, and out he came sputtering and dripping wet paint all over the place. But the workmen had actually done him a favor. The new silver paint matched Homer's original color and pattern: glittering diamond with silver streaks running the length of his body.

After only a few hours in the hospital, Michael had already begun to recover. With his rapid improvement, the doctors predicted he'd be completely well in four days, so Michael's parents could come to the hospital on the fifth day and take him home.

The next day dawned sunny and beautiful. The sandstorm had long since died out, and it was time for the three friends to bid each other goodbye and go their separate ways; Baldazar back to his nest, overlooking the Grand Canyon, Jennie and Homer back to the heliport to fly rescue missions again. Jennie pulled Baldazar close to her and gave him a big parting kiss. Once again, the aristocratic eagle broke out into a bright red blush. "Dear eagle friend," Jennie whispered, "I wish you a safe flight home, and may you always have a speedy tail-wind, and forever soar over your glorious domain!"

Baldazar stammered back, "I'm so happy we met and became pals, Jennie. Take care good care of yourself." Then chuckling Baldazar said, "And keep that Homer 'copter in line!"

Homer and Baldazar smiled at each other, hugged, and bid their tearful farewells. This time, however, they knew that somehow, in the not too distant future, they'd meet once again.

Chapter 12

Jennie and Homer were eager to return to work with the Air Ambulance fleet, but first Jennie needed to test-fly Homer to make sure that all of his controls worked properly. Flying the little 'copter would also shake any remaining sand out of him. So, one clear day while piloting Homer, Jennie took him back into the desert for a test flight. They went through each exercise with excellent precision. Having passed all tests with flying colors, they reported back to the hospital ready for duty.

As Jennie and Homer were landing, Homer was quite surprised to find all the mothers, fathers, children, doctors, and nurses he had worked with awaiting his return. "Why do they all want to see me?" he wondered. The minute they touched down, Jennie jumped out of her pilot's seat, dashed over to the mayor of the city, and whispered something in his ear.

Homer was puzzled, but he soon learned the reason for the whispering.

"Attention! Attention, everyone!" the mayor loudly announced to them, "And especially you, Homer. Listen up. I've got some good news."

"Homer, you've been very brave in your call of duty, and you are, without a doubt, the best Air Ambulance helicopter we've ever had." Homer grinned widely and blushed a bit as the Mayor went on. "So the citizens of this city want to honor you with the highest award a medical chopper can earn." The mayor cleared his throat and continued. "Homer, I take pleasure in presenting you the elegant Red Flying Arrow

Medal."

The beautiful Red Flying Arrow with its gold-tipped white wing stunned Homer! The mayor further explained, "Etched into the center of the arrow is the number 50, representing each of your successful rescue missions. Wear it on your chest proudly, for you've certainly earned it. And congratulations!"

Homer was so overcome with joy and pride that he almost fainted on the spot. He'd never expected to receive such a special award, because he'd just been doing his job the best way he knew how. The mayor then pinned the shiny medal on Homer's chest. The little 'copter felt so grown up now that he had a medal to wear just like Jennie.

The crowd cheered wildly and called to Homer to give a speech, but he was still shaking and practically speechless. Shyly he spoke into the microphone, "Thank you, Mr. Mayor. Thank you so much everyone." Then, waving to all the children in the crowd, Homer called out, "You've made me feel so important. I'll never forget any of you, nor this special day!" Pointing his blades straight at Jennie, he added, "And I couldn't have done it without the greatest lady pilot in the world. Thank you, Jennie!"

Jennie was so proud of Homer, her buttons practically popped off her flying jacket! She congratulated her little 'copter once more on his big day. She thought, "I'm so glad I picked Homer for my medical chopper that spring morning we first met!"

The noonday sun broke through the clouds, and bright rays bounced off Homer's Flying Arrow and his diamond metal skin. He made quite a dazzling sight!

The crowd continued with their applause and celebration, until a loud, roaring sound caught everyone by surprise. The noise grew stronger, and the ground started to shake. Strong air currents swirled around the audience, and some watched helplessly as their hats went sailing off into the air.

An adult helicopter was fast approaching, with powerful blades sharply slapping through the air. The large helicopter created a whipping wind, which stirred up the puffy clouds overhead. Homer was the first to spot its graceful, golden blades. His heart practically leaped out of his chest. It was his mother, Elsa! She looked brilliant even in the cloudy afternoon. All her lights were glowing, and her strobes pierced the sky as they flashed round and

round, like a flaming comet blazing across the sky.

Elsa swooped down right over Homer's head. She was towing a huge, flowing red banner decorated with letters that said: "CONGRATULATIONS, Homer!" With her head held high, Elsa buzzed the crowd to make sure everyone saw her banner. She was so proud of her son she just couldn't help it.

When Elsa flew closer, Homer noticed that his mother's pilot looked familiar. The man's rumpled, sandy-brown hair stuck out from beneath an old, ragged cap.

Homer excitedly thought, "The pilot couldn't be, . . . or, was it possible? Hank!?" The little 'copter strained his eyes to get a better look, and sure enough, he recognized his former pilot and flight teacher, Hank. Homer was thrilled to see his old friend again.

Hank saluted his young pal, flashing his winning grin all the while. Then he motioned for Homer and Jennie to join Elsa and him in flight. The little 'copter could hardly wait to take off! His blades began whirring faster and faster. Jennie had only seconds to make a running dash and bolt into Homer's pilot seat before he lifted off! She fastened her seat belt, and Homer was instantly airborne, racing straight up into Elsa's outstretched arms. The mother helicopter and her son were finally reunited.

It didn't take very long for the four of them, Elsa, Hank, Homer, and Jennie, to begin flying stunts like a precision helicopter team. They delighted the crowd as they performed daring spins, circles, and barrel rolls.

Homer was determined to show off his new flying skills to Hank. He performed fancy flip-flops, cartwheels, and loop-de-loops, accomplishing them all perfectly. "That ought to impress ol' Hank," Homer thought to himself. But Hank's attention had totally shifted to Jennie the moment he'd spotted her at the little copter's controls. He hadn't even noticed Homer's attempts to impress him.

Hank nervously smiled and winked at Jennie. When Jennie noticed Hank's efforts to get her attention, she blushed. Lowering her black eyelashes, she smiled back. Hank then signaled Jennie and Homer to land so they could attend the party prepared in Homer's honor.

Chapter 13

Jennie continued to fly Homer on missions through the Painted Desert and the Grand Canyon wilderness. They stayed very busy rescuing injured and ill children. Homer became a more skillful flier, and as a result, he and Jennie won the award of number one Air Ambulance in the fleet every year.

On many days their trips took them through the massive Grand Canyon. When Baldazar spotted a silver streak flying a zigzag pattern against the sapphire blue sky, he knew his buddy Homer was on his way, and the eagle would frolic between the narrow cliffs, just waiting to show off a new trick.

If there was time, Homer and Baldazar played a game which they named "Stall-Out Tag". The little 'copter was now such an expert flyer that Jennie allowed him to pilot himself without her onboard presence. She didn't mind staying behind, for she knew she'd only get an upset stomach when the pair tried some bizarre stunt.

The two pals chased each other upside-down while performing all kinds of maneuvers just to see who would stall out first. Once in a while, Baldazar would get dizzy first and quit flapping his wings. But usually, Homer was the first to become dizzy. His blades would quit swirling, and he'd plunge downward, dropping like a rock until, eventually, he'd snap himself into level flight again.

Sometimes Baldazar cheated. Quickly doing a Split-S inside-out turn and circling back behind, the eagle would sneak up on Homer and loudly screech: "Got cha!" Baldazar wanted to see if he could spook his friend enough to make paint flecks fly off Homer's nose, like he did the day they first met.

What a pair they were as they romped through the majestic Grand Canyon Park! Soon Homer and Baldazar became one of the canyon's main attractions. Mothers, fathers and especially the children enjoyed watching the twosome's funny stunts. Still, Jennie kept a close eye on the rowdy pair. She warned them to obey the flying rules of the canyon by performing in only one area. If they didn't, the canyon's rangers might kick them out for disturbing the peace.

As evening neared, the shadows thickened and the craggy cliffs began to look like ghostly goblins. Baldazar safely guided Jennie and Homer around the dangerous cliffs out of the canyon. When darkness fell, Homer and Baldazar chased each other's shadows, all the time trying to dodge the beams cast by a full moon. Jennie let Homer take over his controls while she leaned back, relaxed, and enjoyed the ride.

Jennie and Homer had now flown almost one hundred rescue missions, and during each flight the little 'copter had learned a new routine or procedure. He strived to obey Jennie's commands (and his mother's instructions). By minding his pilot, Homer was able to keep the promise he'd made to himself and Hank after their terrible crash. His behavior would always reflect that of a well-behaved, responsible, careful helicopter.

✧⌘✧

One lazy summer afternoon, while parked in a lush meadow partly surrounded by tall pine trees, Homer took a much-deserved rest. Slowly his thoughts turned to the past. He realized how lucky he'd been. During his short lifetime he'd experienced and survived many medical rescues and thrilling adventures. He was also grateful for the loyal friends he'd made along the way. But somehow Homer couldn't help wondering if his future held some new and more exciting adventures.

As he drifted off to sleep, he imagined his engine purring, his blades spinning 'round and 'round, and his nose pointing in a new direction toward the golden setting sun. "Who knows what new journeys and friends might await me far away?" he dreamily thought.

Homer would quickly learn that an awesome journey was awaiting him just around the corner.

53

 # Chapter 14

As Homer continued to dream, he heard a low, rustling sound through the tall pines. A familiar wind gusted against his blades and at once he recognized the Whispering Wind blowing northward. He looked toward the sky and noticed that the clouds were picking up speed as they began to race north. The little 'copter felt a tug in his heart. It seemed to be pulling him in the same direction as the clouds and the wind.

Suddenly, Homer saw blazing streams of light flash across the sky and then disappear into nowhere as quickly as they'd come. The Aurora Borealis! The Northern Lights! He looked around to find out if anyone else had noticed the colorful lights. Baldazar was off in the distance, lazily gliding around the cliffs, while Hank and Jennie were taking a stroll somewhere else in the canyon.

Homer gazed northward again and spun his blades, taking off to get a closer look. To his amazement, a rainbow was arching straight toward him, even though there hadn't been any rain that day. As the rainbow got closer, Homer saw something he'd never seen before. A figure of a woman wrapped up in all the gleaming shades of the rainbow -- yellows, blues, oranges, reds, greens, and purples. The colors flowed behind her and disappeared over the horizon. The lady's hair looked like white clouds, rolling upward and trailing off into the sky. Even though it was daytime, twinkling moonbeams and stars danced around the magical woman's head. Her beautiful gown drifted in the breeze.

But what really captured Homer's attention was the necklace of lightning bolts around the lady's neck. The necklace charged the air with excitement! Homer remembered his experience of getting sky-scorched in the thunderstorm, though he felt oddly at ease in the presence of this mystical woman.

As her gaze fell softly on Homer, she informed him with a voice, which seemed to echo through the cosmos, that her name was Miss Destiny. She held in one hand what looked like Homer's red arrow, and in her other hand a silver bow. The bow was almost as tall as she was, and it gleamed in the sunlight. This incredible being had come to

Homer from the top of the world to deliver a message about his future.

Miss Destiny smiled at Homer, and he felt himself falling under her spell. Her wise silver eyes looked deeply into his as she softly spoke once more, "Watch very carefully, Homer, for my arrow will point the way where your soul yearns to go. You must follow this path of your heart's desire."

Miss Destiny placed her red arrow into the strong bow and lifted it skyward, aiming the arrow toward the North Pole. She pulled the bowstring tightly backward and released the arrow. It shot out of the bow with such force that it sped northward like a rocket and swiftly disappeared. Twang! The bow shook intensely, sending shock waves through the peaceful meadow air. Homer was startled out of his skin!

Miss Destiny explained gently, "Homer, I've watched your progress since you were a newborn 'copter. It's time for you to travel to new lands, learn about the people and creatures that live there, and face new challenges. You'll discover what fortune holds for your future. Good luck, Homer, I'll be keeping an eye on you!"

Then, in a flash, Miss Destiny was gone as quickly as she'd come.

"Follow your heart's desire . . . ?" Homer's head spun. His skids wobbled underneath him as he softly landed. Taking a deep breath and resting a moment, he contemplated what Miss Destiny had said.

Baldazar circled back to look for Homer and find out what his buddy was doing. Right away, the eagle noticed Homer's strange expression, as the 'copter stared northward. Baldazar silently wondered what on earth happened to his pal.

Homer turned around and answered Baldazar's unasked question, "The Northern Lights are calling me toward the great wilderness of Alaska. Miss Destiny has shown me the way with a red flying arrow. Come along with me if you wish, my friend, but I must go on this new journey."

Baldazar staggered backward in shock and disbelief. He stuttered, "Wha-wha-what's the matter with you, Homer? Look, ol' pal, you're *wearing* your red flying arrow, and who or what is 'Miss Destiny'?" The skeptical eagle continued, "We live in a nice, warm climate, Homer, and this entire canyon is our playground. Why would we want to leave such a paradise and go off to freeze in a place we know nothing about?" Baldazar shivered and ruffled his feathers just thinking about it. "Alaska is too close to the North Pole for me!"

"But just think, Baldazar," Homer replied, "what beautiful country is waiting for us to explore and what new creatures we'll meet in the land of the midnight sun! I've heard there are strange beasts that live in Alaska, polar bears, moose, foxes, and mountain goats." Homer could hardly contain his excitement as he went on, "We'll explore giant slabs of solid ice called glaciers, which took thousands of years to form. The glaciers slowly flow down from the mountaintops digging deep valleys along the way, just as the Colorado River carved the Grand Canyon. The ice chunks then plunge into the sea with a thunderous splash!" Homer fell over backward and shouted, "Yippee!" as he imagined a huge glacier cracking into the ocean.

"Still," the stubborn eagle protested, "my tail feathers and bare feet will probably freeze right off!"

"Well, I guess you'll just have to grow thicker feathers, my friend!" Homer teased. Homer hoped he could convince Baldazar to join him. "Did you know that Alaska is home to more eagles than anywhere else on earth?"

"Hmm-m-m-m," Baldazar muttered to himself. "I'll probably be able to rule the skies over this land called Alaska. After all, Alaska can't possibly be very large, can it? It certainly couldn't be as vast and rugged as my Grand Canyon!"

The eagle still questioned Homer, "But what about Jennie and Hank? How will they get along without our help?"

Homer looked around, spotting Hank and Jennie hand in hand taking a romantic evening walk along one of the canyon's winding trails. Pointing one of his blades at the couple, Homer responded, "Look, Baldazar, there they are now. The only things on the minds of those two lovebirds are each other. They will not miss us very much. Jennie and Hank can certainly manage without the two of us tagging along!" Homer coaxed, "So come on, Baldazar, you're a brave eagle. You do want to share new adventures and fun with me, don't you?"

Baldazar thought of all the fun he'd had with Homer, but persisted, thinking of Homer's mother, "But, Homer, what will Elsa think about your running off to Alaska? Will she let you go?"

"My mother knows I've matured into a skillful helicopter," Homer replied. "We'll miss each other, but she'll understand that I must follow my heart's desire. On our way north, we'll stop at the helicopter factory where she lives and tell her we're going to Alaska. We'll also contact Jennie and Hank and ask them to meet us at the factory so all five of us can bid goodbye at the same time." Homer sighed a bit at the thought of having to say goodbye to everyone.

There was no time to lose; the little 'copter had to prepare for his long flight. With or without Baldazar, Homer would be starting on his journey before the moon rose in the night sky.

 # Chapter 15

Homer set his compass direction to north, and started his engine. It roared to life. Homer's silver blades slapped through the air, creating so much lift that he could no longer stay earthbound. The little 'copter darted into the sky!

Though Baldazar hesitated, he couldn't help wondering what adventures, or possibly even disasters, might await his good friend. "Hmm . . ." he thought. "I guess I'm going to be forced to tag along just to keep Homer out of trouble again." Baldazar flapped his strong wings and quickly lifted off the ground. "And didn't he say there were other eagles in Alaska? That's something I've got to see!"

Homer glanced around and was delighted to see Baldazar flying right behind him. At that moment, a song about Alaska, which Homer had heard years ago, popped into his head. He began singing, "North to Alaska, go north, the rush is on." He then belted out the tune even louder, "North to Alaska . . . Go north, the rush is on!"

Baldazar complained to Homer, "Do you realize that the gusts from your tail rotor ripped loose several of my feathers and they've gone sailing off into space somewhere, never to be found again?! Now I'll freeze to death for sure in that . . . uh . . . what is the name of that icebox place . . . Alaska? Land of the Midnight Sun?" A confused expression crossed the eagle's face, "And if there's that much sun, explain to me why it's so cold . . . huh?"

Homer didn't say a word. He just smiled to himself and started humming North to Alaska again. Shortly Baldazar joined in. Soon they were both singing the tune together. The pair contentedly winged along, not even turning to look back.

೪೪

The sun began setting in the west, turning the cliffs of the Grand Canyon into tall, spiraling shadows appearing as castles of old. Jennie and Hank gazed skyward, admiring the brilliantly lit horizon.

Jennie spotted the North Star and sighed, "Oh, look, Hank. The bright North Star!"

"Yes, I see it." Hank replied. "It looks like a big, sparkling diamond. It reminds me of Homer's shiny silver color."

Jennie's thoughts turned to Homer and Baldazar. She hadn't seen them all day. She began searching the canyon's rims for the pair. Jennie asked Hank, "I wonder where my plucky 'copter and that smart-aleck eagle are? Which dangerous cliffs are they cavorting around this evening?"

The sun had now fallen below the horizon, and the sky was fast becoming dark. As they looked northward Jennie and Hank barely spotted in the distance what appeared to be two flying objects, some sort of spinning silver streak and maybe a huge bird, winging along side by side. Jennie and Hank heard a faint tune in the distance, which sounded like "North to Alaska."

Jennie stammered, "Quick, Hank, hand me your binoculars." Jennie pointed the strong magnifying glasses toward the north and barely spotted Homer and Baldazar. "There they are," she happily cried. "But, Hank, they're flying north without us! Where could they be going?"

Hank smirked a bit, "Judging by the tune, I'd say probably . . . north, to Alaska."

Jennie giggled, but her smile soon gave way to a concerned expression. "Could they be attempting such a long trip to a strange place without any help or guidance? Alaska is full of dangers: huge glaciers, towering mountains, raging blizzards, bad-tempered moose, and hungry, grizzly bears. Homer and Baldazar have never been away from Arizona."

"Hank," Jennie frantically continued, "we've got to catch those two right away! What shall we do?"

Hank thought a moment. "I'll bet Homer would let his mother know if he were flying to Alaska. Let's contact Elsa right now and find out. Maybe she can help."

Jennie grabbed the communications radio microphone and quickly dialed Elsa's air frequency number. When Elsa answered, Jennie hurriedly told her, "Elsa, did you know Homer and Baldazar are flying north. Hank and I think they're heading for Alaska. Did Homer tell you he was leaving the Grand Canyon?"

Elsa was surprised and upset. "No, Jennie," she replied. "What is that mischievous son of mine and scamp of an eagle up to now?"

Elsa then volunteered to immediately fly to the canyon, pick up Jennie and Hank so the three of them could start after Homer and Baldazar as soon as possible.

 # Chapter 16

Homer had changed his direction and was now headed for the helicopter factory. Upon his arrival, he flew overhead, searching the ground for Elsa, but couldn't find her anywhere. His mind raced. "Where is my mother? Has something happened to her? Did she fly off somewhere?"

Homer and Baldazar quickly landed.

Off in the distance, Elsa had keenly spotted Homer and Baldazar on the ground. Pointing one of her blades at them, she excitedly shouted to Hank and Jennie, "There they are! We've found those two rascals!"

Elsa flew to the helicopter factory in a flash! Homer and Baldazar were so busy looking for her on the ground they didn't notice her approaching them from above. Elsa promptly brought her engine to a grinding stop. Ggrrrrind! Kerplunk! She landed so close to Homer that her blades missed hitting his by mere inches. Elsa's blast of swirling air flipped Homer and Baldazar on their sides. Stunned, they slowly picked themselves up and turned around, astonished to find Elsa, Jennie and Hank giggling down at them.

Homer and Baldazar were still shaking, but extremely happy to see Elsa and their two friends. Homer shouted, "Oh, Mom! I'm so glad you came to the factory and found us!"

Elsa distressfully questioned Homer, "Why are you and Baldazar headed north in such a big hurry?"

Homer began making up an explanation, but then he remembered Miss Destiny's advice to follow his heart's desire. So Homer gathered his courage and told Elsa, Hank, and Jennie the story of Miss Destiny's visit to him, and his plans to head north to Alaska to face new challenges.

When Homer finished telling his story, Elsa, Hank and Jennie were flabbergasted. They wondered if he'd just imagined the whole, wild tale. However, they saw Homer's enthusiasm, and how important this journey was to him.

Elsa, Hank and Jennie asked Baldazar, "Why are you journeying all the way to Alaska with Homer?"

The eagle nobly answered, "Somebody's got to go along to keep him out of trouble. Who better than I?"

Homer continued, "I'm sorry if Baldazar and I upset you three by leaving so suddenly. We weren't going to go without saying goodbye."

Elsa slowly sighed. Then, in an understanding voice, she replied, "Yes, Homer, it's alright. You're more mature, experienced and stronger now. You're old enough to explore new lands and deal with new challenges." Elsa smiled over at Jennie and Hank. "Although the three of us will miss you terribly, we want you to become the helicopter you're destined to be." Jennie and Hank nodded in agreement.

Hank chuckled, "Well, Homer, ol' buddy, I guess we can no longer call you 'our little 'copter'."

Elsa looked at the helicopter factory and fondly remarked, "And here we are, Homer, back at the place where you were born. Do you remember when you were a young, frisky helicopter and flew behind me, zigging and zagging bouncing up and down?"

Homer laughed. "Yes. I can't believe I was once that young and wobbly! I was so lucky to have you for a mom, and Hank and Jennie as my flight instructors. How can I ever thank each of you for the lessons you taught me?"

Jennie replied, "Your love and loyalty are all we need, Homer. Maybe we can visit you in Alaska sometime." Hank and Elsa nodded in agreement.

Homer delightedly exclaimed: "That'd be great!"

Looking into Baldazar's eyes, Elsa said, "Keep my Homer safe. We're trusting him to your care."

"You can count on me," replied Baldazar with a new air of responsibility and purpose.

Elsa, Jennie and Hank each had a parting gift for Homer, mementos to remember them by. Elsa gave him a pair of gold flight wings. From Hank Homer received silver wings, and from Jennie a pair of turquoise wings.

The little 'copter wore all the medals proudly.

"Thank you," mom, Hank and Jennie, Homer said. "I'll never forget any of you nor the adventures we've shared."

Baldazar was a bit jealous and squawked: "Well, what about me?!"

Jennie giggled and gave Baldazar a big kiss on the cheek! The cocky eagle brightly blushed red once again and then fell right over! Plop! Everyone laughed, as Baldazar lay dazed on the ground with a goofy grin on his beak.

 # Chapter 17

The hours had quickly sped by. It was time for Homer and Baldazar to start their journey. Homer fondly looked at Elsa, Jennie and Hank, his big, emerald eyes glistened with tears. It was hard for him to leave.

Seeing Homer's sad face, Jennie piped up, "Why don't Elsa, Hank and I fly along with you and Baldazar to the Golden Gate Bridge? It's a famous landmark, and many people have bid farewell by its rocky shores. What better place for us to say goodbye?"

A wide grin crossed the little 'copter's face and he gleefully took the lead. "The Golden Gate Bridge it is! Let's go!"

Homer was airborne at once with Baldazar flying alongside. Hank and Jennie jumped into Elsa's cockpit. Elsa lifted off in a flash. She quickly caught up with Homer. Their gold and silver colors blazed through the sky.

The five of them flew over the barren desert. After two hours flight the massive Boulder Dam came into view. The high dam holds back the Colorado River, creating Lake Mead in Nevada. Homer shuddered as he remembered his crash in the treacherous river in the bottom of Grand Canyon.

On the fliers journeyed, across the vast Death Valley Desert, over the snow-capped peaks of the Sierra-Nevada Mountains, and down into the green valleys of California.

Finally the white buildings of San Francisco appeared in the distance. The five travelers caught their first glimpse of the Golden Gate Bridge. Soon they spotted two massive steel pillars, soaring 800 feet into the sky, below which the Pacific Ocean stretched westward for thousands of miles.

Elsa, Homer, and Baldazar gracefully circled the wide bridge. The passengers, on ships below, admired the two beautiful helicopters and the magnificent bald eagle flying high overhead.

⋘⋙

Elsa soon landed on one of the bridge's pillars. She motioned Homer and Baldazar to join her and the two flew over.

They all said their final good-byes. From Elsa's cockpit Hank saluted Homer once more, and Jennie blew a kiss to the 'copter and another to Baldazar.

Elsa tightly hugged Homer and said, "You and Baldazar will remain deep in our hearts."

Elsa lifted off, swiftly circling the Golden Gate Bridge. As she passed Homer and Baldazar, she rocked her blades in one last loving wing-wag-wave. Then the three flew south, back toward the Grand Canyon.

Homer watched his mother, Hank and Jennie until they disappeared over the horizon. Homer loved them so much his eyes watered with huge teardrops, but his desire to fly north tugged at him stronger than ever.

Homer turned to Baldazar and asked, "Ya' ready for our journey, ol' buddy?"

Baldazar replied, "You bet, . . . let's go. I can hardly wait!"

Homer mischievously grinned as he said, "Okay! Then let's begin our voyage with a kick, Baldazar. If I use the bridge's highest cables like a slingshot, we can head off on our trip with a burst of speed!"

"Oh, no . . ." the big eagle squawked, "What if you flub your take off and we end up in the ocean?"

Homer replied, "But we're beginning a new adventure, Baldazar, so let's start with a ride we'll never forget!"

"And we may never live through," Baldazar muttered.

Homer instructed the leery eagle, "Hang on to my wing. Here we go!"

Before Baldazar could protest, Homer wrapped his skids around two of the tallest cables and pulled them back, stretching the wires tight. He started his engine revving at full power. His blades whirred faster and faster, whipping the air into a strong whirlwind, pulling the cables back farther and farther, until . . . Snap! Pop! TWANG-G-G! Homer cut his engine, and the giant cables shot them north at great speed! The two hurtled through the air laughing and screeching with joy. Baldazar let go of Homer's wing, gliding along the side of his pal once more. Homer quickly restarted his engine in midair to keep himself in flight.

Baldazar breathlessly shouted, "Yippee! We're finally on our way!"

Homer gleefully yelled, "Next stop, Alaska!"

☙❧

That evening the people living along Homer and Baldazar's route watched as a quick, silver helicopter and a magnificent bald eagle winged their way toward the Northern Lights. The villagers also heard a strange tune, echoing across the landscape. Something like . . . "North to Alaska, . . . Go north the rush is on."

THE END

Julie W. Buscher

Author's Biography:

Children's author, Julie (Julia) W. Buscher was born and raised in rural Central Utah.

Having graduated from business college, she has worked as a paralegal secretary, and is an experienced business writer. She has traveled the country, and lived in the western United States all her life. She enjoys writing poems, humorous articles, and engages in other creative endeavors.
Her other interests include genealogy and playing the piano.

"Homer the Helicopter Grand Canyon Adventures" is her first book.

Presently, she lives in Brighton, Colorado with her husband of 30 years, where they regularly fly their vintage Cessna 180 aircraft.

Author's Website: www.HomerTheHelicopter.com

70

C.M.Rogers

Illustrator's Biography:

Though born in Illinois, he has lived most of his life in central and Northern Colorado. Having graduated from Colorado State University in 2005, he works now as an illustrator, photographer, typesetter, print and digital media designer and sculptor in Fort Collins, Colorado.

Illustrator's Website: www.WhiteCatGraphics.com